Orphan Escape

By: Tori Lavan

*For Azriella, Tsofia, Ashira,
and Amitai who helped me
create this story*

Chapter 1

Maxine was a young girl who lived in London. She was very happy and very kind to everyone, and she had one big wish: to find her family. Sadly, when she was very young, her parents died from a late-night car crash on an icy road, and she was soon after transferred to an orphanage. The orphanage was not a bad place. Most of the other girls living there were nice, and they often went on day trips around their wonderful city. But still, Maxine dreamed of more. Though she was happy to live in a safe space and have a warm supper every evening, the orphanage did look a bit old, and the food looked a bit too much like mold.

Maxine's best friend in all of London was her brown teddy bear that she had since she was a baby, and she brought him everywhere. For all of the orphanage's day trips, she carried him around in her old, blue backpack with his head peeking out. But Maxine had one big secret she never told anyone: her teddy could talk. When she was all alone, he would come to life and they would chat about everything. Mainly they spoke about finding her family. Teddy remembered long ago, when Maxine was just a baby, her parents talking about an aunt who lived in the city. Maxine never met this aunt, but always wondered about her, and why she never visited.

"I think it's time," the little girl said when her and Teddy were alone.

"On the next weekend trip?" Teddy asked.

"Yes," Maxine said with a little fear, but much more confidence.

"What do we do first?" Teddy asked.

"We need to go to the library."

The orphanage had lots of books and lots of toys, but no televisions, tablets, or computers. Maxine and Teddy both knew that they would have to do some research before they could chart a route to find her aunt.

"Okay!" exclaimed Teddy, "We'll go along with the group as normal, and then during lunch we can sneak away!"

"Yes, that will be the perfect time," Maxine responded thoughtfully.

"Um... and where are we going again for the trip?" Teddy asked.

"You've already forgotten? We're going to the zoo!"

"Oh, right, yes," Teddy said nervously.

"Are you scared?" Maxine asked.

"Well, the animals are quite big there, aren't they?"

"Yes, but don't worry, you will stay in my backpack and I won't let any of them near you!"

"Okay. Thank you," Teddy said, relieved.

All the girls of the orphanage's trip to the zoo was bright and early the next morning. As the girls prepared for the upcoming trip, Teddy sat on the bed looking just like any other stuffed animal. Many of the other orphans had stuffed animals as well, but none of them could talk like Teddy (He tried again and again to speak with Peggy the Bunny, but she never said a peep).

The orphan girls were laying out their clothes for the next morning and putting snacks into their bags. Maxine on the other hand very discreetly packed a few more essentials: a map of London, her old library card, and some money she saved, just in case. All of the girls were chatting excitedly about the zoo. Maxine was a bit too nervous to join in. After packing, she laid on her bed with her teddy, feeling that soon she would be one step closer to finding her family.

Chapter 2

At 7:00 o'clock sharp, Maxine woke up with the rest of the orphanage, put on her uniform, placed her red day-trip cap over her plaits, and slid her backpack up her arms, with Teddy's head peeking out at the top. Before leaving, everyone went downstairs to the dining hall and was served porridge. The porridge was a funny color, but Maxine forced herself to eat so she would have strength for her upcoming adventure. She wondered what sort of breakfast she would eat when she lived with her aunt. Maxine once saw pictures of a big breakfast in a book, which had plates of things she never tried before. The picture of pancakes looked the most delicious. She hoped that her aunt would make her pancakes.

Soon after breakfast, all the girls of the orphanage went to board the coach, which was heading to the

London Zoo. Maxine put Teddy and her backpack on the seat next to her. Teddy, seeing that Maxine was quite nervous, whispered in the quietest voice, "Everything will be okay! We will find your aunt!" Maxine nodded and then smiled. The journey ahead was risky, but she felt courage from the thought of the happiness she would feel when she finally had a family.

Once they arrived, there were a few hours to go until lunchtime. At the

London Zoo, the caretakers led the orphans around all of the enclosures. Maxine and Teddy enjoyed viewing the animals. They saw the tall giraffes, the colorful snakes, and the giant, bumpy camels. Teddy was shocked to see some big, brown bears.

"They look just like me," Teddy said. "Do they talk?" The bears just growled.

For lunch the girls of the orphanage headed to the park alongside the zoo to sit and eat in the trimmed green grass.

The park was very busy on that Sunday afternoon, perfect for their escape. All of the orphans stood in a queue, and after the caretakers handed out paper lunch bags, the girls each found a place in the grass to eat. When it was Maxine's turn, she took a lunch bag, and started walking towards her friends. There were a group of teenagers walking just behind her. Teddy made sure to watch the caretakers.

"Act natural. They are looking this way," he said with a soft voice. Maxine tried not to look nervous. "Okay," Teddy whispered, "They are speaking with one of the girls. Run!"

Maxine knew this was her moment. The group of teenagers caught up to her and she used them as a shield to quickly change course. She ran away from the group of orphan girls sitting on the grass, straight to the path, ripping off her cap so she wouldn't be spotted, snaking her way through the crowds of people, and sprinting to the entrance of the park. She dug into her backpack, opened her map to double-check her route, and made her way forward. Running up the street, she looked around and knew that she was in Camden Town.

Chapter 3

"We did it, Teddy!" Maxine exclaimed. "We're in Camden!"

"Yes!" Teddy shouted. "Now, where is the library?" he asked.

"I think it's this way," she replied.

Maxine and Teddy walked through the vibrant, busy streets of Camden. There were lots of colors, noises, and great smells. As they were walking, Maxine realized that she *was* a bit hungry after all. She looked into the lunch bag that she was still grasping in her left hand. Inside was a sandwich. She investigated further. The sandwich was two pieces of bread and a sliver of lettuce. Not quite a sandwich after all.

"Teddy?" Maxine started.

"Yes?" he responded.

"Do you think we have time to stop for lunch?"

"I think we can spare a few minutes."

Maxine was very pleased to pick up a nice, warm lunch from the Camden Market. She bounced around every stall and chose what looked the most delicious. With her monthly allowances that she's been saving, Maxine bought a big burger and fries. Her and Teddy sat at some picnic tables, and the sun broke through the clouds. Maxine never had a lunch that tasted this good.

After her meal, Maxine investigated her map, and set off to the library. "This way, Teddy."

Upon arrival, Maxine walked inside and found a place at the computer. She pulled out her old library card and set Teddy on her lap. Slowly, she typed her library card number and password to log in. When the home screen flickered on, Maxine wasn't too sure how to start searching. She had only used a computer a few times in her life.

"Hmm... where is, uh, Gog... uh... Google?" Maxine asked herself.

"Do you need help?" asked a voice next to her. The voice came from a boy about her age.

"Um, do you know how to find Google?" she asked.

"Yes, of course," the boy said, laughing. "It's right here." He clicked a few times with the mouse and a window came up. "Just type in there what you need."

"Thank you!" Maxine said with a smile.

"He talks funny," Teddy said in a whisper.

"Shh," Maxine shushed back.

"What?" The boy asked, turning his head from his computer.

"Um, you don't talk like the people here in London," she said.

"Yeah. I'm from New York!"

"Wow!"

"Where are you from?" he asked.

"Here. I've lived here forever, in an orphanage since I was a baby."

"What are you doing here in Camden?"

"I'm looking for someone."

"Do you need any help?" he asked. Maxine wasn't sure if she should let someone else join their adventure.

"Say, yes!" Teddy whispered, interrupting her thoughts. "He knows all about Google!"

"Okay. I'd love some help," she responded.

"Cool!" he said happily, but Maxine thought of one question first.

"What's your name?" she asked.

“It’s Tai.”

Chapter 4

"Nice to meet you Tai! I'm Maxine. We... I appreciate your help," Maxine said, smiling at her new friend.

"Nice to meet you, too. Who is it you're looking for?" Tai responded.

"I'm trying to find my aunt. She's the only family member I've got."

"Wow. Let's see what we can find. First, type in her name, then you can scroll through the pages to see if anything looks important," Tai said, pointing to different parts of the computer screen.

"Thank you!" Maxine said with true honesty.

Tai smiled and went back to sit at the computer station next to theirs, focusing again on his work, but glancing here and there at Maxine in case she needed any help. Teddy took this opportunity to whisper to her, "Okay, type in her name."

"Got it!" Maxine said. She put in the letters of the name which would hopefully be the key to the next step of their adventure:

REBECCA CONGITU

As instructed by Tai, she pressed the "search" button. Immediately, a bunch of headlines appeared listing titles such as "Congu, congita, and conguita." She clicked to the next page and then the next, worried that nothing would come up.

"You'll find her," said Teddy with encouragement.

"I hope," Maxine responded in a quiet voice.

Finally a headline caught Maxine's attention. It seemed to be a website of old newspaper articles. One said:

Local Music Teacher, Rebecca Congitu Holds Charity Concert for North London Community

She clicked on the page and was immediately greeted by an old, grainy photo of a lady in front of a house. Maxine squinted and looked closely. The lady on the screen looked a lot like the picture of her mother. A loud noise drew Maxine away from the computer screen. There was a big printer at the end of the table, and she saw Tai clicking on a printer icon. Funny looking pieces of paper were spewing out of the machine. He pulled them out of the printer and stacked them next to himself. Maxine copied what Tai did on his computer screen, and printed the newspaper article she found. She saw it a minute later in the printer tray, took it, folded it, and put it safely into her backpack.

"Did you find her?" Tai asked.

"We have a lead," Maxine responded with a smile.

"When do we have to go back?" Teddy whispered in her ear so Tai couldn't hear. Maxine looked at the nearest clock.

Tai noticed and asked, "What are you doing after this?"

"Well, I have to get back soon to my group."

"How soon?"

"Not too soon."

"Do you want to go somewhere with me?" Tai asked.

"Sure. I just need to be back at Regent's Park by 6:00pm."

"No problem. We can take the tube afterwards."

"The tube?" Teddy whispered, a bit anxious.

"I've never been on the tube," Maxine said.

"You will love it," Tai assured. "Let's go!"

Chapter 5

As they exited the library, Tai was grasping his funny black and white papers, and began jogging through the streets.

"I'm running a bit late!" he called back to Maxine. With a giggle, she went running after him.

"Where are we going?" she asked him in a shout.

"We need to find the station!"

Maxine, Tai, and Teddy sitting in the backpack, ran up the busy Camden streets until they approached the end of the sidewalk. Maxine looked up to see a big blue sign and big white letters:

CAMDEN TOWN STATION

"Watch this!" called Tai. Maxine looked as Tai ran through the station, and ducked under the partitions. He motioned for Maxine to follow him.

"He's a bit of a troublemaker, isn't he?" Teddy asked.

Maxine shrugged, looked nervously at security, and followed him under the gates. He took her hand and they started running down the left side of the escalator, almost crashing into the other people on the way down. Across the corridor to their platform, they could see the train slowing to a stop.

"Faster!" Tai called. Just in the nick of time, Maxine and Tai jumped into the train and the doors closed behind them.

"I almost got squished!" Teddy cried in despair.

The kids were out of breath but began laughing as the train began to zoom away.

"I guess this isn't so bad," said Teddy.

"What's our stop?" Maxine asked as they found two free seats.

"We're going to Waterloo."

"And then?"

"You'll see."

When the loudspeaker announced "Waterloo Station," the two friends and Teddy jumped off the train and left the station. Tai led the group through colorful and busy streets. Maxine was delighted to see all of the restaurants, shops, skateboarders, and grand buildings. The group approached the "Royal Festival Hall." Maxine didn't know at all what this place was. Why was there a whole building dedicated to being a hall? And why did they hold festivals there? She thought that maybe Tai was taking her to a party. Maxine didn't remember ever going to a real party. At the orphanage, when it was somebody's birthday, they would watch a movie, sing "Happy Birthday," and get a biscuit after dinner. Cake was never allowed at the orphanage. The caretakers always said it was too much of a luxury. But Maxine always wanted to try cake. The pictures of cakes she'd seen looked so colorful and amazing. She wondered if this Hall had cake.

Tai pushed through the big, grand doors, and a man waiting in the foyer said, "Hello, Tai. You're just in time."

"Perfect," said Tai. "I brought a friend to watch."

"Great," he responded and then looked at Maxine. "Hello, I'm Walt. I hope you enjoy the rehearsal."

"Rehearsal?" she asked.

Tai was grinning.

"You can come with me this way to take your seat," Walt told Maxine. He then led her forward, opened some doors, and revealed a big, grand theater with red everywhere, rows and rows of seats, and a brightly lit stage.

"Wow," both Maxine and Teddy said at the same time.

"Find a place anywhere," Walt said to her. "Tai will meet with you after."

Maxine, in awe, walked towards the stage and found a desirable seat at its foot. She put her backpack in the seat next to her with Teddy facing front so he could also see. Moments later, a bunch of musicians carrying different instruments started spilling into the stage, chatting with each other, and playing odd tones on their instruments. It was a big cloud of sound; a mixture of music and chatter. Then, Maxine spotted a familiar face. Tai came out carrying a violin. He waved to Maxine and took his seat, right in the front. He placed some slightly crumpled pieces of paper onto the music stand facing him. Maxine suddenly realized that the funny shapes on the pages Tai printed at the library were music notes.

"It's music!" she said. "Tai is a musician!"

Chapter 6

As Maxine and Teddy sat at the foot of the grand stage, the concert hall suddenly dimmed, and each performer on stage was lit with a golden light.

"All right, everybody," the conductor said, standing in the front and center of all of the musicians. "Let's play through the second movement again. Our concert is tomorrow night! Tai, are you ready?"

"Yes, sir," Tai responded.

Suddenly the orchestra began to play. The wind instruments introduced a melody and then Tai stood up. When he started bowing his violin, both Teddy and Maxine's jaws dropped. He led the orchestra in a beautiful and emotional sound. Maxine never heard any music like this before. She was frozen, eyes lit, watching the musicians, and taking in the wonderfully crafted sound. She was also happy to see her new friend playing so well and enjoying the performance. Maxine and Teddy sat silently in their seats, looking here and there, and enjoyed every moment of the rehearsal hour.

"Sounds great guys. See you tomorrow night," the conductor said at the finish.

All of the musicians resumed their chatter and began packing up their instruments. Tai carefully placed his violin in his case, zipped it up, and jumped off the stage.

"Did you like it?" Tai asked with excitement.

"Yes! We... I thought it was amazing! I've never heard music like this before. Thanks for letting me listen!" Maxine responded.

"Of course. There's a concert tomorrow night if you want to come."

"I'm not sure if I will be able to leave the orphanage."

"Well, if you can make it..." Tai grabbed a sheet of his funny, musical paper and ripped off a piece of it. He then took his pencil and scribbled on the page. "Here's my phone number. Call me if you are able to come."

"Thanks!" Maxine said, smiling.

"It's almost 4:00pm," whispered Teddy.

"Right. I should head back to Regent's Park."

"Okay. I'll take you to the tube station. I have to go back to my hotel for violin lessons, but I'll show you which train to take and where to get off."

Tai, Maxine, and Teddy in his bag, walked slowly back to the tube station, not particularly wanting to go home after their adventure. At the platform, they faced each other, ready to say goodbye.

"Thanks for everything, Tai. I hope we will see each other again soon."

"Yes. It was fun! Try to come to my concert tomorrow night!"

Maxine laughed. "I'll see what I can do."

They gave each other a hug and parted ways. Maxine and Teddy boarded their train and were a bit nervous to find their way without Tai. Maxine was very careful to listen each time the announcer spoke to hear him call, "Regent's Park Station." At the cue, she hopped out of the train and ascended to the street to search for the group. Luckily, Maxine saw a sea of familiar red hats standing in a line, ready to board their coach. She sneakily approached, following a crowd of people, and made her way into the group without anyone's notice. Soon she was in her seat and heading back to the orphanage. Maxine and Teddy both fell asleep on the coach, as it was a very eventful day.

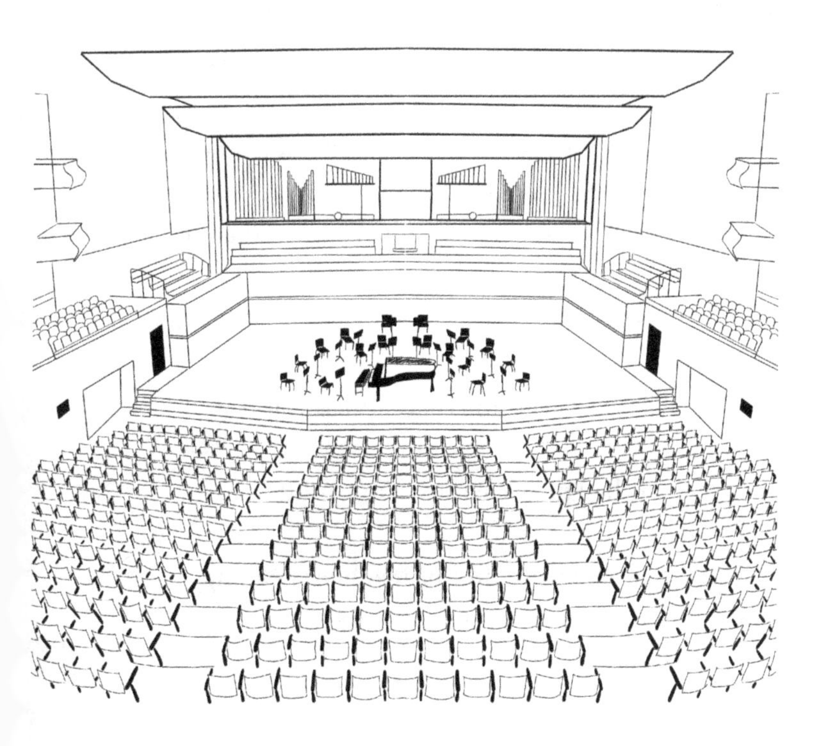

Chapter 7

The next morning, just like every regular, boring day at the orphanage, Maxine woke up at the normal time and went to eat her usual, dreary breakfast. Unlike the other girls, Maxine was very anxious for the morning break to start so that she could study the newspaper article she printed at the library. Maxine ate her cold porridge quickly and went to her first lessons. She couldn't concentrate on her teacher speaking about ancient history. What is important to her now is what she will soon discover. Her family.

Once they were released from lessons for their break, Maxine ran upstairs. Teddy was waiting for her there.

"Teddy, I have 15 minutes. We have to read through the article!"

Teddy jumped down from the bed and started digging through the old, blue backpack. He pulled out the folded sheet of paper.

"Here it is!" he exclaimed.

The two best friends spread out the paper and sat on the bed, looking down at the article. Maxine reread the title:

Local Music Teacher, Rebecca Congitu Holds Charity Concert for North London Community

She then read out loud to Teddy,

Local music teacher, Ms. Congitu mixes music and charity to put together the best concert that the Hampstead community has ever seen. After months of volunteer music lessons for children around the North London area, Ms. Congitu assembled an excellent ensemble of students who performed a spectacular concert to raise money for poor children in the city. Pictured here is Ms. Congitu in front of her Hampstead home where she teaches her lessons.

"Hmm," said Teddy in response. "She lives in Hampstead, but where?"

Maxine looked closely at the picture, knowing that something was there to give her another clue. She just couldn't find what it was.

"I don't know, Teddy," she said, studying every single detail of the picture. Then she saw something...

"Look Teddy," she finally said. "There's a street address here."

"And a house number!" he exclaimed.

"But what is it?"

"Hold on a moment," Teddy said, jumping to the floor, and diving under the bed of one of Maxine's fellow orphans. "Here it is!" Teddy shouted from under. He came out holding a magnifying glass. "I saw Penny hiding this under her bed a few days ago."

"Wow, Teddy. Thanks!" Maxine said. She took the magnifying glass and looked closely.

"I think it says… hmm… 36… Pilgrim's Lane?"

"Let me see," Teddy said, holding the magnifying glass to his face. "I think you're right."

"Teddy, we have to go!" Maxine said with excitement.

"Let's go now!" He responded.

"I'll go and tell the teachers I am not feeling well. I received top marks on the recent exams, so they won't mind me missing a lesson. In the meantime, pack up what we need," she said and ran outside the room to find her teacher.

"Yes, ma'am!" Teddy shouted.

Teddy began running around the room trying to figure out how to get ready. What would they need?

"Coats!" Teddy said. "What else? Biscuits! Well, maybe not. Passport to show who we are? Yes. Money? Yes." He put a few more things into the backpack right as Maxine returned.

"Okay, Teddy. I am free from my lessons. Let's go!"

While everyone was back in the classroom, Maxine and Teddy quickly and quietly snuck out of their room, ran through the hallway past the kitchen, and into the dining room which had am exit to the side of the building. They quietly closed the door and went running down the streets towards a bus stop. Soon, they were off to Hampstead Heath.

Chapter 8

As the bus approached Hampstead Heath, it seemed that Maxine and Teddy were entering a forest. Beautiful, green trees surrounded them. Maxine hopped off of the bus and exclaimed, "Wow, Teddy. It's so beautiful here."

"Do you think bears live here?" Teddy asked.

"I'm not sure," Maxine responded. She started heading down

the hill, following the other people who exited the bus. After a few minutes of walking, Maxine and Teddy reached the high street. "We must be close," she said.

Going along their route, Maxine and Teddy saw a man in a kiosk selling magazines and coffee. Maxine bravely stepped up to meet him.

"Do you know where Pilgrim's Lane is?" she asked.

"Yes, love. Continue down the hill and take a left," he said.

"Thank you!" she responded and continued on.

"How far is it?" Teddy asked with his head peeking out of the backpack.

"I believe we're almost there," she said happily.

Maxine and Teddy continued down the hill and were greeted with a sign that read "Pilgrim's Lane." They took a left where the sign indicated, and searched for the house number. Maxine walked and walked, looking at every single house, locating the numbers, and feeling anxious as she got closer and closer. Finally, her heart was beating wildly as she was standing in front of the house numbered "36."

"Here it is Teddy," she said in a quiet voice, and stood still facing the house's front.

"Go knock on the door!" Teddy urged her.

Maxine started walking towards the front door with her legs feeling like stones, three times their weight as normal. She pressed the doorbell, heard a ring, and waited. As the door began cracking open, her heart jumped around even quicker, and then she faced the lady of the house.

Chapter 9

“Hello?” asked an old lady that Maxine sadly did not recognize. Maxine was a bit flustered.

“Um, hello. I’m looking for Rebecca Congitu.”

“Oh, Ms. Congitu. Yes. Great musician,” the old lady answered in a high voice, staring up at the sky. Maxine curiously glanced at the sky too, not seeing anything in particular.

"Do you know where she is?" Maxine asked again.

"I haven't heard that name in a while. I haven't heard from Rebecca in a while, in fact. This was her house, as you must know. She sold it to me. She lives in New York now. Moved there about eight years ago, or maybe nine now. I've been here for a while..." The lady said, chattering on and on. Maxine's heart sank. New York was so far away.

"Do you have her phone number? Or address?" Maxine asked desperately.

"I do have her address. You see, I was doing a spring clean and found some old letters left behind in a box, shoved into the back of a cabinet… strange place indeed… must have missed them it the move. Didn't look like much to me, but I had the sense to save them. Funny enough, she called to ask for them a few years back. I sent them off to New York. I have her address written down somewhere. Come in, I can find it for you."

Maxine entered the Hampstead house and a cat came over to greet her. He purred, asked to be pet, and then stared suspiciously at Teddy.

"It's just in my address book here. Let me see, I'll write it down for you. And then, you must want a biscuit I expect?" the old lady wrote down a New York address and to Maxine's surprise, passed her a handful of biscuits. "Here you go."

"Thank you. Thank you so much!" Maxine said.

"Not a problem my dear, now thanks for stopping by. I expect you need to return to school, and I must give lunch to the cats. Good luck! Tell Rebecca I said hello," she said as she escorted Maxine and Teddy out.

"That was a bit odd," Teddy said as the door closed behind them.

"It doesn't matter because we have my aunt's true address now!"

"But what should we do? It's all the way in New York."

"Tai is from New York! Let's call him and see if he has any advice."

"Good idea!"

Maxine recalled seeing a telephone box on the way over, and headed that direction. She found the bright red structure and opened the door to dial her friend.

"Teddy," Maxine said, "could you look for Tai's phone number in the backpack?

"No problem," Teddy replied and then disappeared into the bag. Maxine felt the bag shake a bit and then Teddy came out grasping the piece of torn off sheet music. "Here it is!" he said.

"Thanks. Now, we need 60 pence."

"We have some change in the backpack. Let me see," Teddy said, diving back inside the bag and returning with a paw full of shiny coins. "Here's the 60 pence."

Maxine put the coin into the machine and Teddy climbed out of the backpack and closed the door behind them. He stood on the floor looking up at his friend. The phone began to ring.

"Hello?" Answered Tai. Maxine recognized his voice right away.

"Hello, Tai!"

"Hey, how's it going? Did you find your aunt?"

"I just found her old house but learned that she is currently living in New York. We… I wanted to ask for advice on how to get there."

"Great! You can fly there with me tonight. If you want, I can get you a plane ticket. Hold on."

Maxine heard a bump as Tai dropped his phone, and then two muffled voices sounded through the speaker. She looked over.

"He's going to get us a plane ticket!" She whispered to Teddy. "But, Teddy, how much do you think it costs?"

"Well, it takes £1.50 to get to the city center by bus. That takes about an hour. How long does it take to get to New York?"

"I'm not sure. I think one of my teachers told us how long because she went there on holiday. Maybe five or six hours?"

"Well, then, it must be about £10."

"Right, we definitely have enough for that."

"Hello?" She heard Tai ask on the phone.

"I'm here!"

"All right. My manager Walt got you a seat next to mine. I'm leaving right after the concert."

"Thank you, Tai! Could I pay you back? I have some money from my allowance."

Tai laughed, "Don't worry about it. It's nothing, I have a bunch of frequent flyer miles. Can you come to my concert tonight?"

"Yes! I will go see the concert and be ready to leave after!"

"Perfect! Let me give you the flight number so you can print your boarding pass, and once you get to the concert hall, just say your name at the door and they will give you your tickets there." Tai then named a series of letters and numbers. Maxine repeated them out loud so that Teddy could scribbled them down.

"Thank you so much, Tai! I'll see you tonight!"

"See ya!"

Maxine was very happy that she would soon be in New York, but also realized that she had a few things to do before she would be able to leave.

"Okay, Teddy, we need to go print our boarding pass, get to the concert hall, and make sure we are ready to go to New York. I don't know if we can go back to the orphanage, it's too risky."

"Here's what we can do," Teddy explained. "You go buy some clothes and I'll go back to the library to print the boarding pass. Then we can meet at the concert hall."

"Are you sure Teddy?" Maxine asked, worried about Teddy going off alone.

"I will be okay," Teddy said.

"Here," said Maxine, "wear this so no one suspects anything." She took off her coat, her favorite hat with two ducks on it, her red scarf, and put it on Teddy, covering his ears and his nose. Teddy looked really funny with the coat going way past his feet, and only his eyes visible. "Okay, Teddy, we need to get going. I'll see you at the concert hall!"

Teddy ran off in one direction and Maxine started in another. It was a long day for the pair so far, but Maxine was really, really brightened by the thought that she might never have to return to the orphanage again.

Chapter 10

It was just about to be dark and the air was becoming crisp and chilly, but Maxine was warm with excitement. She was wearing a new dress she bought, and her bag was full of essentials she found on Oxford Street, purchased with her allowance money that she saved up. All of the girls got a monthly allowance to be used for different things like ordering new books and buying trinkets on their school trips. But all those years, something told Maxine to save her money. She never bought a school trip souvenir, and she borrowed dusty, old books from the orphanage's library. Because of this, she had enough money to buy some essentials for her New York trip, and would be able to pay for a taxi to her aunt's house. She remembered in one of the library books seeing a yellow taxicab in New York City. She was looking forward to riding one herself.

Maxine shivered a bit in the cold and saw a small figure running towards her. It was Teddy.

"I got it!" he called at her. She just smiled, watching him run in her coat, which was very much too big for him. She gave him a hug when he approached.

"How did it go?" she asked.

"All went well, but they thought I was a toddler. There was a singing group at the library. I had to dodge the librarian and quickly print out the boarding pass. Then this baby who kept saying 'quack quack' tried to steal your duck hat. Once I had the boarding pass, I was able to finally sneak away!"

Teddy took off her coat and hat, and climbed back into the backpack. Maxine straightened out her new dress and walked inside, waited in the ticket queue, said her name, and entered the concert hall. The ushers led her up to a special box right in the corner by the stage. It was as if she was floating over the whole concert hall. All of the musicians they saw yesterday began to stream into the stage, though this time they were dressed up in black with bowties and high heels. Maxine smiled when she saw Tai in his concert clothes. The conductor entered the stage and the hall thundered with applause. The orchestra began to play the most magical sounds, and Maxine and Teddy, looking down upon the musicians, enjoyed every single second.

When the concert ended, Maxine and Teddy were jumping up and down and clapping the loudest. The hall was noisy with applause, and everyone admired Tai for his amazing solos. As the audience began exiting the hall, Maxine and Teddy stayed in the box and looked down as the musicians were packing up their instruments. Tai was jumping and waving at them to get Maxine's attention.

"Meet me in the lobby!" he shouted up at them. Then he ran off behind the stage.

Maxine with Teddy in her backpack set off to the lobby. There, all of the audience members were chatting, laughing, and drinking sparkly drinks. There were a few TVs hanging from the walls, and Maxine saw a flash of a really

odd picture. It was a picture of her.

"Nine year old girl goes missing

from a London orphanage," Maxine

heard the newscaster say. Her body

filled with fear. There was a picture of

the orphanage where she lived for so

many years, and she saw an interviewer speaking with one of her teachers.

"She was fine this morning, but after first break, went to her room feeling sick. We haven't seen her since then." Maxine was in shock, watching the people she grew up with on the news.

"Did she run away or was she kidnapped? If you see this girl, call the police immediately," the newscaster declared.

"Oh no," said Teddy.

Maxine didn't know what to do or say, and then Tai appeared holding his violin in one hand and his suitcase in the other.

"We have to go!" she shouted. "They're looking for me! I'll never be able to find my aunt if I have to go back to the orphanage!"

"I saw your picture on the TV in the dressing room. Don't worry. We'll leave now. No one can catch us!"

Tai grabbed Maxine's hand and they went racing off to the tube station. Alongside Tai, Maxine ran under the partitions and hopped on the train with her head kept low so that no one would recognize her. They were heading towards the Heathrow airport.

Chapter 11

Heathrow airport was bumbling with people on that cold, dark, evening, but Maxine was only concerned with being safely sat on the airplane. She had her boarding pass in hand, and her backpack with Teddy in it went through the security sensors. If she weren't so nervous, she would be laughing at the funny look Teddy had on his face. When she walked through the metal detectors, she was worried that the security guards would recognize her from the news. But they only asked, "Are you two alone?"

"I fly alone all the time," Tai replied confidently. "And this is my friend. We have our boarding passes!"

The security guards were amused by Tai standing tall and confidently in his bowtie.

"All right then, safe travels you two."

Maxine felt a bit more secure after getting into the airport without any problems.

"First we need to find our gate, and then we should get some dinner. I'm starving!" Tai said.

"Sounds good to me," she responded. Her and Tai skipped around the airport looking for the "New York" departure sign. Their flight was leaving late into the night. Maxine should have been sleepy, her bedtime long past, but the excitement of the day and the nervousness of what she saw on the news kept her awake. Once they found where their flight departed, Tai went off to grab some sandwiches.

"Hey," said the voice of a stranger. "Are you the girl from the news?"

Maxine faced him with big eyes, worried that this could be the moment that changed her future. What if he called the police? What if they stopped her from entering the airplane? What if she never found her aunt? She would go back to living the same life, day after day in the orphanage, never knowing if she truly had a family.

But then Maxine decided that her fate was up to her and her alone. She would use the same confidence that Tai always had. Nothing could get in her way.

"Of course not! I am not an orphan!" she then stormed off to an empty chair far from the man, but where Tai could still find her. Soon after, Tai returned with two delicious looking sandwiches, and Maxine ate happily with no more fear left inside her. She was going to have an excellent dinner, a fun flight, and a great trip to New York.

"That looks yummy," she heard Teddy whisper in her ear.

Not long after finishing their supper, they were ready to board.

Maxine had her old passport from when she was a baby, and showed it to the nice lady at the desk.

"Have a great flight!" the lady said to her. Maxine and Tai had big, comfy seats in the front with pillows, blankets, and TV's with loads of different movies to choose from.

"Wow!" said Maxine. "I haven't seen any of these!"

"Really?" Tai responded. "This one is my favorite! And this one!" Tai began talking on and on about all of the movies, which ones he did and didn't like. The two friends decided to watch one together. The flight was soon to depart and the air hostess came to their seat.

"Hello, you two," she said in an American accent. "Wanna change your seats to be beds?" she asked.

"Sure," Tai responded.

She set up the beds for them and then pointed to a special compartment.

"We have popcorn and candy in here. Call me if you need anything!"

"Thanks," said Tai. He pulled out some of the candy. "Want some?"

"Yes!" Maxine responded, cozy in her bed with Teddy next to her. "I've never had these!"

"What! Then you need some more," Tai pulled out all of the candy and threw it on her lap, and then the two were laughing. The airplane started moving and barreling forward.

"Woo!" Tai shouted. They were laughing and laughing more and more as they zoomed into the air.

"Have you ever flown before?" Tai asked her.

"No, I don't think so," Maxine responded.

"Let me see your passport," Tai said. Maxine pulled her passport out of her bag and Tai began studying each page.

"Look here." Tai showed her a page and a faded stamp. "You've been to New York before!"

"I have?" Maxine asked with disbelief.

"The stamp is right here!" Tai said.

Maxine took back her passport and looked at a faded stamp on one of the pages. It was hard to read, but she could see that it was marked the year she was a baby. She'd been to America before. It must have been to visit her family. After seeing this, she was filled with confidence that this would be the trip that would change her life.

Chapter 12

At some point in the journey, Maxine and Tai both fell asleep. After a few hours, they woke up to sunshine streaming into their windows. Maxine was very confused about where she was when she woke up. Then she saw Tai and her memories of the previous day flooded back.

"Wow, we're here," Tai said. And it turned out that they were already on the ground.

The other passengers were moving around and grabbing their luggage. Maxine grabbed her backpack and put Teddy back in along with some leftover candy. Maxine and Tai left the plane, got their passports stamped, and headed outside to the busy New York morning. The airport entrance was lined with yellow taxicabs.

"Can I show you something before you go find your aunt?" Tai asked. "It's my favorite place in New York."

"Okay," Maxine replied. She knew that now she was free and had all the time in the world. "Let's go!"

The two friends jumped into a yellow cab, with Teddy in the backpack, and the violin swinging around. Tai shouted at the driver, "Empire State Building, please!"

"Sure thing, son," the cab driver shouted back. They were off like a rocket, whirling through the streets, and straight into the city. Soon they were surrounded by buildings touching the blue sky, living amongst the clouds.

"Wow!" said Maxine. "These buildings are huge!"

"Yep! This is New York!" Tai said with a smile.

The taxicab took them in front of one of the tallest buildings, with a point on top poking the heavens. Tai and Maxine jumped out of the cab and ran towards the building.

"Are we allowed inside?" Maxine asked in a shout.

"Of course!" said Tai.

Maxine and Tai entered a crowded elevator and shot straight up. They exited into a balcony that looked over the whole city. Maxine was in awe. She could see every single building lit up by the rising sun, making a beautiful scene of this great American city.

"This is my favorite place on Earth," Tai said. "And I'm so happy you came with me. I don't have a lot of friends because I'm always in rehearsals and playing concerts. I love it, but it's nice to finally have someone to hang out with."

"Thanks for taking me," Maxine responded. "I've never had such a fun time in my life, running around London, seeing your concert, going to New York! I finally feel free, and I can't wait to find my family. All thanks to you."

"Ah, no problem," Tai said.

All of a sudden, Maxine was feeling brave.

"Tai? Can I show you something?"

"Sure."

"It's a bit strange, but... You'll see." She pulled out Teddy. I want you to meet Teddy. She saw Teddy's eyes grow big.

"Hi Teddy," Tai said with a smile, not suspecting anything.

"Hi," Teddy responded.

"Whoah!" Tai shouted and jumped back. Then he started laughing.

"I knew something was strange about that bear!" The three of them laughed together.

"I've known Teddy all my life," Maxine said. "He's my best friend and I wanted you to know my secret."

"Amazing!" Tai said. Teddy was quite shy, never having talked to anyone aside from Maxine.

"Nice to meet you, Teddy," Tai said.

"We're so happy you're helping us, Tai," Teddy said in a quiet voice.

Maxine, Tai, and Teddy enjoyed the morning looking at the views from the building. After, they went back to street level for a breakfast bagel. It was the perfect New York morning.

"Well, I need to head to a rehearsal soon. You can go find your aunt, and maybe we can meet somewhere later for pizza," Tai said.

"Sure!" Said Maxine. Tai wrote down a time and the address to his favorite pizza place in the city.

"I'll grab a cab for you and then I'll take the subway," He said. Tai nearly ran into the street flagging down a cab for Maxine.

"See you later!" He said.

"See you!" She called back.

She gave the cab driver her aunt's address and rocketed off into the city.

Chapter 13

This was the moment. The taxi driver stopped in front of a building, and Maxine knew in her heart that her aunt was inside. Now, she was truly moments away from finding her family. She would no longer be "the orphan girl." Just a regular girl living a happy life with people around her who loved her. No more cold porridge, no more old library books, no more uneventful birthdays. She rang the bell and she felt

Teddy shaking in her bag. She was shaking a bit too.

The door screeched open, and the lady before her looked very familiar, but was someone she never met before. She had red hair just like Maxine, and eyes that looked like her mother's. It was the 10-years-older version of the lady in the newspaper article. Maxine was looking at her aunt.

"Hello?" she asked. "Are you one of my new students?"

"No. I'm your niece," Maxine replied shakily.

"What do you mean?" she asked, confused.

"I'm Claire and Ben's daughter. I'm Maxine."

"Wha-? How?" Rebecca began muttering unintelligible things.

Her aunt stood in shock but then dropped to the floor with her hands in her face. Maxine grew even more worried.

"What's wrong?" Teddy whispered.

Maxine didn't know what to say. Her aunt lifted her head, tears in her eyes.

"What do you mean?" she asked with an abrupt tone.

"I'm Maxine. I've been living in an orphanage since I was a baby after my parents died. I've been trying to find you." As Maxine said this, a few tears dropped down. She was overwhelmed with emotion and worried about her aunt's reaction. Why didn't she understand?

"I thought you were dead, too. They said you were gone," her aunt declared with her voice wobbling. She then grabbed Maxine in a great, warm hug. At this point, Maxine was fully crying too. Not because she was sad, but because she finally felt at home.

Soon after Maxine was sitting in a cozy kitchen with a cup of hot chocolate after a nice, warm bath. She couldn't believe what she learned today. After being escorted into the house, her aunt calmed down and told her everything.

"I was living in Hampstead, near your family. When I was traveling to play a concert, I heard the news. They said you didn't make it either. I couldn't handle what I heard, and I couldn't return to London, not even for the funeral. I've just been traveling to different countries, teaching music, and trying not to think about what happened. We finally moved to New York a few years ago. Your mother and I are from New York. Did you know that? You came here when you were a baby. Right before they died. I haven't been to London since the accident. I'm so sorry I never returned. I could have found you sooner. I'm so sorry." Her aunt began crying again. "But how did you find me?" she asked.

"Well, I've been living at the orphanage, but I escaped and found an old newspaper article which had the address of your old house. Then the woman there told me where you lived in New York! Oh, and I had a friend help me get here!" Maxine explained.

"You escaped?" her aunt asked, shocked.

"Yes," she said, a bit scared, but her aunt just started laughing and Maxine laughed with her.

"Did the lady living in my old house tell you about the letters?" Rebecca asked.

"Not much. Just that she found them," Maxine responded.

"Hold on a minute," Rebecca said, and left the room.

"I like her." Teddy whispered to Maxine when they were all alone.

"Me, too," she responded. But no words could express the happiness she now felt.

"Found them!" they heard Rebecca shout before entering the room. She was carrying an old box. At the table, she opened the lid, and took out a stack of envelopes.

"These are from your parents. They always sent me letters when I was traveling or when they were abroad, and with lots of baby pictures, of course," Rebecca said, opening a letter. "Look here."

Maxine took the photograph her aunt handed her. It was a picture of her parents and her as a baby. She had never seen this picture before.

"I was in a panic when I thought I lost them! I was thankful for Mrs. Violet who moved in my old house. For sending them back to me."

Rebecca and Maxine spent the next hour reading through the old letters. Maxine loved hearing the stories about her mom and dad that she never knew before. She felt warmth and joy aside her aunt, connecting with her parents who she only had for a year of her life. The reminiscent hour was interrupted by a ring of the doorbell.

"That will be my son," her aunt said, and walked off toward the door.

"I have a cousin!" Maxine told Teddy.

"I wonder what he's like?" Teddy asked.

Then to their complete surprise, Rebecca Congitu reentered the kitchen alongside... Tai!

"TAI!" Maxine shouted.

"WHAT?" Tai shouted back.

"You know each other?" Rebecca asked.

"He's the friend who's been helping me!" Maxine shouted.

"She's the new friend I told you about!" Tai shouted.

They both started laughing uncontrollably, and hugged each other.

"We're cousins!" they said together.

Epilogue

Just as she suspected, Maxine now had such a different life. She had a family of two great people, Rebecca and Tai. She lived in a beautiful house as her aunt immediately told her she must move in. She had great dinners every night, stacks of pancakes for breakfast, birthday cake, lots of new movies and books to read, an amazing city to discover, and she was even learning music now. Her aunt insisted she learn, and told her all about how her parents were musicians too, both playing the viola and cello in symphonies, just like she saw Tai play. She chose to play cello just like her mother. After her great adventure through two magical cities, Maxine had a really full, wonderful, musical life with her two best friends Tai and Teddy.

The End

About the Author

Tori Lavan is a composer from California who loves to travel and read many books. Her time spent with children inspired this story (as a bribe for the kids to get ready for school on time). Orphan Escape reflects her love of London, New York, and classical music, and she hopes that readers enjoy going along the adventure with Maxine, Tai, and Teddy.

CPSIA information can be obtained
at www.ICGtesting.com
Printed in the USA
LVHW031101100921
697437LV00004B/405